The Magic Snow-Bird

...and other stories

Enid Blyton

The Magic Snow-Bird

...and other stories

Bounty
Books

Published in 2015 by Bounty Books,
a division of Octopus Publishing Group Ltd,
Carmelite House,
50 Victoria Embankment,
London EC4Y 0DZ
www.octopusbooks.co.uk

An Hachette UK Company
www.hachette.co.uk
Enid Blyton ® Text copyright © 2015 Hodder & Stoughton Ltd.
Illustrations copyright © 2015 Octopus Publishing Group Ltd.
Layout copyright © 2015 Octopus Publishing Group Ltd.

Illustrated by Jane Etteridge.

ISBN: 978-0-75372-939-7

A CIP catalogue record for this book is available from the
British Library.

CONTENTS

How Derry the Dormouse Lost his Secret

Once upon a time Derry the dormouse hid a nice little store of cherry-stones in the hole of a hollow tree. He was so pleased with them that he went to look at them every day. Sometimes he nibbled one, and when he came to the kernel inside he ate it all up.

But he couldn't keep his secret to himself. When he met Bright-Eyes the squirrel, he called to him:

'Bend your head down, Bright-Eyes, and I will tell you something. I have a store of cherry-stones in the hollow tree! It is nice to have a secret like that!'

Bright-Eyes listened, and then leapt up the trunk of a tree. At the top he found Screech the jay, looking very colourful in the sun.

'Bend your head down, Screech, and I will tell you something,' he said. 'Someone has a store of cherry-stones in the hollow tree. There is a secret for you if you like!'

Screech opened his beak and made a noise like his name. Then he flew off and came down in a field where Four-Paws the hare was nibbling grass.

'Bend your head down, Four-Paws,

and I will tell you something,' said Screech. 'Someone has a store of cherry-stones in the hollow tree. There is a secret for you if you like!'

Four-Paws listened eagerly and then went bounding over the field. It wasn't long before he met Mowdie the mole.

'Bend your head down, Mowdie, and I will tell you something,' he said. 'Someone has a store of cherry-stones in the hollow tree. There is a secret for you if you like!'

Mowdie listened and then ran off in a

9

hurry. Soon she saw Grunt the hedge-hog, and she spoke to him.

'Bend your head down, Grunt, and I will tell you something,' she said. 'Someone has a store of cherry-stones in the hollow tree. There is a secret for you if you like!'

Grunt listened, and then went on his way down the ditch. Soon he met Flicker the robin, and he called to him.

'Bend your head down, Flicker, and I

will tell you something,' he said. 'Someone has a store of cherry-stones in the
hollow tree. There is a secret for you if
you like!'

Flicker listened and flew off. When
he saw Fuff-Fuff the long-tailed field-
mouse, he called to him.

'Bend your head down, Fuff-Fuff,
and I will tell you something,' said
Flicker. 'Someone has a store of cherry-
stones in the hollow tree. There is a
secret for you if you like!'

Fuff-Fuff listened and ran off. He
went straight to the hollow tree, and
there he found the store of cherry-
stones. Then, quickly and quietly, he
carried them one by one in his mouth to
where he had his home in a hole in the

bank of the field.

That evening Screech, Four-Paws, Mowdie, Grunt and Flicker all met together with Derry, and with one accord they began to tell him his secret.

'Oh, Derry,' they said. 'We have a secret to tell you. Someone has a store of cherry-stones in the hollow tree.'

'Why, that is *my* secret!' cried Derry the dormouse, in surprise. 'How is it you all know it? But, since you do know it, come and I will show you my store of cherry-stones in the hollow tree.'

He took them to the tree, and they all peered in. Alas and alack, the hole was empty! No cherry-stones were to be seen at all.

'Oh! Oh!' wept Derry the dormouse. 'Now my secret is gone. My cherry-stones are stolen. If I had only kept my secret, I should have kept my stones too! Where, oh where, is my little store of cherry-stones that I gathered so carefully from the orchard down the valley?'

But no one knew. Only Fuff-Fuff

could have told him, and Fuff-Fuff wasn't going to. He was sitting in his hole, nibbling through the cherry-stones to get at the kernels inside. Oh, naughty little Fuff-Fuff!

The Surprising Blackberry

'Let's go blackberrying,' said Thomas to Wendy. 'There are heaps of berries on the hill above the village.'

'All right,' said Wendy. 'I'll get the baskets.'

'Bring me back enough to make Daddy a blackberry pie!' said their mother. 'He loves that, and will be so pleased to see it.'

So the children promised to bring back their baskets quite full, so that Daddy could have a pie that evening. Off they went, carrying their baskets in which their mother had put sandwiches for them.

It was a long climb up the hill, and when at last they reached the big stretch of blackberry bushes, they were both tired.

'Shall we eat our sandwiches now?' said Wendy. 'Then we can pick blackberries until it is time to go home.'

'Yes,' said Thomas. So they sat down and ate their sandwiches. That emptied their baskets, so they at once set to work to pick the blackberries. What a lot there were! Great big, juicy ones, as black as could be! The children ate a lot, and filled their baskets as well.

When they had got a good load, and their baskets were almost running over with the berries, they sat down for a rest. The sun was very hot indeed, and they found a nice shady place under a tree. They put their baskets on the grass in the shade and lay

down beside them.

They were both tired, and in a few moments they were fast asleep. Wendy woke up first and dug Thomas in the ribs.

'Wake up,' she said. 'We've both been asleep! Hadn't we better start for home?'

'Yes,' said Thomas, rubbing his eyes. He put out his hand for his basket, and then stared in the utmost surprise! For it was quite empty!

Wendy looked at hers too — and that was quite empty as well! The two children didn't know what to make of it. They were very upset.

'Someone has been along and stolen our blackberries,' said Thomas, in a temper. 'Oh, what a mean thing to do! Now Daddy won't have any pie for supper!'

'Who can it be?' asked Wendy.

The two children stood up and looked all around them. There was no sign of anyone. Then suddenly Thomas sniffed the air.

'Smell, Wendy!' he said. 'Sniff the air!'

Wendy sniffed. Then she turned to Thomas in excitement.

'That's the smell of blackberry pie!' she said. 'Someone's making it quite near here — and I guess it is with our blackberries!'

The children went in the direction of the delicious smell. It got stronger and stronger, and suddenly they came to a little door set deep in the hillside. It was

The Surprising Blackberry

open, and from inside came the smell of blackberry pie. Someone was singing a little song, and when Wendy peeped in, she saw a pixie standing by a table, setting it with knives and forks.

Thomas went boldly into the tiny room, and startled the pixie so much that he dropped a knife and fork with a great clatter.

'Where did you get those blackberries for your pie?' asked Thomas. 'Did you take them out of our baskets?'

Before the pixie could answer a lovely fairy came in through the open door too.

'Is dinner ready?' she began to ask – and then she saw Thomas and stared in surprise.

'What do you want here?' she said.

'If you please,' said Thomas, 'I came to find out if the blackberries cooking in that pie over there were stolen from our baskets whilst we were asleep.'

'Oh, how dreadful!' said the fairy. She turned to the pixie and spoke to him sternly.

'Slyfoot,' she said, 'have you been up to your tricks again? Did you take those blackberries from these children, or did you pick them, as I told you to?'

'I t-t-took them from their b-b-baskets,' stammered the pixie, going very red. 'You see, I hadn't t-t-time to pick them, and—'

'You very naughty little pixie!' cried the fairy. 'Go out of the room this minute, and put yourself straight to bed!'

The pixie burst into tears and left the room howling. The fairy turned to Thomas and said how sorry she was.

'He is a very naughty fellow,' she said. 'I am always having to punish him. May I pay you for the blackberries he stole?'

'Oh no,' said Thomas, politely. 'Please don't trouble any further.'

'You see, they were for Daddy's blackberry pie tonight,' explained Wendy, who had come into the little room to see what was happening. 'He will be disappointed, but we can easily get some more tomorrow.'

'Oh dear!'said the fairy, in distress. 'I do hate anyone to be disappointed. Ah, wait a minute! I know what I can do! I have a magic blackberry somewhere which will be just the thing for you!'

She hunted in some drawers and at last brought out a small, hard blackberry which was not quite ripe. She gave it to Thomas and told him what to do with it.

'You put it on a dish and say:

> 'Blackberry small,
> Please will you try
> To make yourself
> Into a blackberry pie?

'Then you will see something surprising!' she said. Thomas took the berry and thanked her very much. Then they said goodbye and ran off down the hillside, carrying their baskets with them.

'What an adventure, Wendy!' said Thomas. 'I do wonder what will happen when we say the magic rhyme.'

Mother was very disappointed when she saw that their baskets were quite empty. But when she heard about their adventure, she could hardly believe her ears.

'Here's Daddy,' she said. 'Now put the blackberry on a dish, and see what happens.'

So, with everybody watching, Thomas put the little blackberry into a big pie-dish and said,

> 'Blackberry small,
> Please will you try
> To make yourself
> Into a blackberry pie?'

Nothing happened at first. Then the blackberry suddenly swelled, and broke into six pieces, each of which became a berry, black and juicy. Then they all swelled and six more came from each. This went on till the pie-dish was full. Then, suddenly, so quickly that no one saw how it happened, the dish was covered with a lovely crust.

The Surprising Blackberry

Then steam began to rise from the pie, and the crust turned a golden brown.

It was ready to eat!

'Good gracious!' cried Father. 'That is quite the most wonderful thing I've ever seen. We must keep that magic blackberry and use it lots of times!'

But, of course, nobody knew which of the blackberries was the right one! Mother cut the pie and peered inside to see the little hard berry but they couldn't. It was cooked along with the rest!

'Never mind!' said Father. 'Let's eat the lovely pie!'

So they did – and they all said it was the best they had ever tasted in their lives. By the time they had finished there wasn't even a crumb left!

'Tomorrow I'll go with you to see that little house in the hillside,' said Father.

But wasn't it disappointing, when they got there the little door had vanished, and though they hunted everywhere, up and down the hill, they couldn't find it again.

'Never mind, we've had the pie!' said Thomas. '*Wasn't* that blackberry surprising? I wonder which of us ate it!' But none of them ever knew!

The Magic Snow-Bird

It was holiday time, when mothers were giving lots of parties. Jim and Mollie had been asked to a great many, and they were very much looking forward to them. They had been to one, and then a dreadful thing happened! Baby caught chicken-pox – and that meant no more parties for Mollie and Jim in case they caught it too.

Wasn't it unlucky! They were *so* disappointed. Mollie cried, and Jim nearly did, but not quite. There was to be a Christmas tree at the next two parties they had been asked to, and now they would miss all the fun. It was too bad.

'Well, it's no use making a fuss,' said Mother. 'You can't go and you must be brave about it. We are all very sorry for you. Look, I believe it's going to snow! You will be able to play at snowballing soon.'

Sure enough, the snow was falling thickly. Mollie and Jim went to the window and watched it. It came down like big goose feathers, soft and silent. Soon the garden was covered in a white sheet.

The next morning there was about fifteen centimetres of snow everywhere, and the two children shouted with delight.

'We'll build a snowman! We'll snowball the paper-boy! We'll build a little snow-hut!'

'Put on your wellington boots, your thick coats, and woolly caps,' said Mother. 'Then you can go and do what you like.'

So out they went. How lovely it was! Their feet made big marks in the snow, and when they kicked it, it flew up into the air like powder.

'Let's build a snowman first,' said Jim. So they began. They made big

The Magic Snow-Bird

balls of snow by rolling them down the lawn. They got bigger and bigger, and then, when they were nice and large, Jim used them for the snowman's body.

They put a hat on his head, and a pipe in his mouth, stones down his front for buttons, and old gloves on his snowy hands. He did look funny. Mother laughed when she saw him.

'Now what shall we make,' asked Jim. 'What about a snow-bird, Mollie? Do you remember how we made a bird at school out of clay? It was quite easy. Let's make a big one out of snow!'

'Yes, nobody makes snow-birds!' said Mollie. 'How surprised everyone will be!'

So they began. First they made a round body. Then they put the bird's long neck on. After that they made a head with a beak of wood sticking out. Then they gave him a long tail sweeping down to the ground. He stood on two wooden legs, and had two stones for eyes, so he looked very grand indeed.

'Isn't he wonderful!' cried Mollie.

'Just look at him, Jim! Let's call Daddy and Mummy, they'll be so surprised.'

They went to call them, and soon Father and Mother came out into the garden to see the bird. They thought he was magnificent.

Now, just at that very moment a bright blue kingfisher flashed by. He had come from the river, and was going to a nice pool he knew, which he hoped would not be quite frozen over. As he passed over the snow-bird, he dropped one of his blue feathers. It floated down, and stuck in the snow-bird's head, just on the top, so that he looked as if he had a funny little crest.

'Oh, look!' cried Mollie. 'He's got a blue feather on his top-knot! Doesn't he look funny!'

'Leave it,' said Mother. 'Kingfishers' feathers are lucky.'

So they left it, and went in to dinner. It was still there when they went out to play afterwards. This time they made a nice little hut with a door and window. It was just big enough for the two of

them. Jim and Mollie were sorry when the sun went and the garden began to get dark.

'We shall have to go in to tea soon,' said Jim, looking out of the little snow-window. Then he suddenly said 'Oh!' and sat very still, staring hard.

'What's the matter?' said Mollie.

'Sh!' said Jim, in a whisper. 'Keep still. I saw something strange.'

'Oh, *what*?' asked Mollie. 'Quick, tell me.'

'I thought I saw the snow-bird stretch its wings,' said Jim, in astonishment. 'But look – he's quite still now, isn't he, Mollie?'

'Yes, quite,' said Mollie. 'Oh, Jim! Did you really see that?'

'Well, I *thought* I did,' said Jim. 'Let's watch and see if he moves again.'

They watched quietly for a few minutes and then they were called in to tea, and in they had to go. They told Mother what they thought had happened, and she laughed.

'Well, maybe that kingfisher's

feather has put some magic into the snow-bird,' she said. 'Everybody knows that there's something magical about kingfishers' feathers.'

'That must be it!' thought the two children. 'What a funny thing!'

After tea they went to the nursery window, and tried to see out into the garden. It was dark, but they could just make out the snowman, the snow-hut and the snow-bird. As they peered out into the darkness, they heard a peculiar noise.

'It sounds like some sort of bird,' said Mollie. '*Could* it be the snow-bird whistling, Jim? It's a kind of singing-whistling noise all mixed up.'

'Let's go and see,' said Jim. So they scrambled down from the window, and ran to put on their coats. Then they slipped out into the garden.

'Yes, it *is* the snow-bird!' said Jim, in astonishment. 'It must be magic, Mollie.'

They went close up to him. He gleamed white in the darkness, and his two stoney eyes shone brightly.

'Look!' said Jim, 'he's opening and shutting his wings! He's come alive!'

The snow-bird stared at them solemnly. He stood first on one leg, and then on the other. Then he flapped his

white wings, and stood on tiptoe.

'Hello, hello, hello!' he said. 'It's nice of you to come and see me. I was just feeling rather lonely.'

'Are you magic?' asked Mollie, who was just a bit frightened.

'I am rather,' answered the bird. 'It's all because of that kingfisher's feather, you know. It's very lucky, and it's very magic. It would make anything come alive!'

'Are you going to fly away?' asked Jim. 'Where will you go to, if you do?'

'All snow-birds, snowmen, and snow-animals belong to the country of the North Wind,' said the bird. 'It's a fine land too. It's where Santa Claus lives, you know. The toys are made there by goblins and dwarfs, the Christmas trees grow there, already decorated with toys—'

'What! Do they grow with toys on them?' cried the children. '*We've* only seen the kind that you buy, and dress up with toys yourself.'

'Pooh,' said the bird. 'Those are

stupid. You should just see the ones that grow out in the country of the North Wind! I shall see some tonight, if I go.'

'We were going to some parties where there would be lovely Christmas trees covered with toys,' said Jim. 'But now Baby's got chicken-pox, and we can't. I do wish we could go with you, and see some trees growing with toys already on them.'

'Well, why not?' said the bird, spreading its white wings. 'There's plenty of room on my back, isn't there? You can both sit there comfortably, whilst I fly. I'll bring you back safely enough.'

'Oh!' cried both children in delight. 'What an adventure!'

'You may find me rather cold to sit on,' said the bird. 'I'm made of snow, you know. You'd better get a cushion to put on my back, then you won't feel cold.'

Jim ran to the house and fetched a big cushion from his bedroom. He popped it on the snow-bird's back, and then he and Mollie climbed on. The bird spread its wings, and then *whoosh*! he rose into the air!

Mollie and Jim held on tight. Their hearts were beating very fast, but they were enjoying themselves enormously.

The bird went at a fearful rate, and the children had to pull their woolly caps well down over their ears. They looked downwards, but the earth was too dark for them to see anything except little spots of light here and there.

After a long time, the bird turned its head round to them.

'Nearly there!' he said. 'Isn't this fun!'

'Yes!' shouted the children. 'Oh look! Everything is getting lighter. The sun is rising!'

'Yes, we've gone so fast and far that we've met him again!' said the bird. 'I'm going to land now, so hold tight. You'll be able to see everything quite well soon.'

Down he went, and down. Then *bump*! he landed on the snowy ground. Jim and Mollie jumped off his back. There was sunlight everywhere and they could see everything clearly.

'We haven't much time,' said the snow-bird. 'This is where the goblins live who make the rocking-horses for you.'

He took the children to some big caves in a nearby hill, and Jim and Mollie saw hundreds of tiny goblins busily hammering, painting and putting rockers and manes on fine rocking-horses. The funny thing was

that the horses seemed alive, and neighed and kicked and stamped all the time.

The children watched in astonishment. Then the snow-bird asked if they might have a ride on one of the horses, and the goblins said yes, certainly. So up they jumped, and off went the horse with them, rocking all over the cave. Jim and Mollie loved it.

Then the bird took them to where the dolls' houses were being built by tiny pixies. The pixies lived in them, and Mollie thought it was lovely to see them sitting at the little tables on tiny chairs, peeping out of the windows, and sleeping in the small beds.

'Now hurry up, or we shan't have time to see the Christmas trees growing,' said the snow-bird. 'Jump on my back again. They're not far away.'

He took them to a huge field spread with snow. In it were rows and rows of Christmas trees, some very tiny, some bigger, and some so big that Jim and Mollie had to bend their heads back to

The Magic Snow-Bird

see the tops.

'Look at the tiny ones,' said Jim.
'They have got little buds on them. Are
the buds going to grow into toys, snow-
bird?'

'Yes, they are,' said the snow-bird.
'Look at the next row. They are bigger
still.'

The children looked. They went
from row to row, and saw the toys
getting bigger and bigger as the trees
grew in size. At first they were tight
little buds. Then they loosened a little,
and Jim and Mollie could make out a
tiny doll, or a little engine. The next
size trees had toys a little bigger, and
the largest trees of all were dressed
with the biggest, loveliest things you
could imagine! Fairy dolls, big books,
fine engines, great boxes of soldiers,
footballs and all kinds of things hung
there!

'Will the little trees grow into big
trees like this, with all the toys the
right size?' asked Mollie.

'Of course,' said the snow-bird. 'Then

people buy them. Look, this tree is bought by someone. It has a label on it. It is to be fetched tomorrow.'

Jim read the label.

FOR JACK BROWN'S PARTY, it said.

'Oh!' cried Mollie. 'Why, that's the party we were going to tomorrow! To think that this lovely tree is going to be there! Oh, I *wish* we were going!'

Her eyes filled with tears, and the snow-bird was terribly upset.

'Don't, please don't,' he begged. 'Look,

you shall have a little Christmas tree seed for your own. Plant it, and it will grow into a good size by next Christmas!'

'And have toys on, too?' asked Mollie.

'Certainly,' said the bird. He pressed something into Mollie's hand. She took it. It was a tiny silver ball, the sort you see on Christmas cakes.

'Thank you,' said Mollie. 'I'll be sure to plant it carefully. What fun to have a Christmas tree of my own, with toys and everything on!'

'Now it's time we went back,' said the snow-bird. 'It's nearly seven o'clock by your time, and your mother will want to put you to bed. Jump up again, my dears.'

Up they climbed, and once more the snow-bird flew back into the darkness, leaving the sun far behind him. The wind blew hard, and the children held on tightly, afraid of being blown off.

'Pff! Isn't the wind strong!' cried the bird. Then suddenly he gave a terrible cry.

'Oh, whatever is it?' cried Mollie.

'The wind has blown away the king-isher's feather on my head!' cried the bird. 'The magic's going out of me! I shall soon be nothing but a bird made of snow. Oh, oh, I hope you get home safely before that happens!'

He flew more and more slowly, and it seemed to the frightened children as if he were becoming colder and colder. At last he gave a pant, and fell to earth. The children tumbled off, and rolled on the snowy ground. Then they picked themselves up, and looked round.

'Are we home, or not?' asked Jim. 'I can't see the snow-hut or the snow-man, can you, Mollie?'

'No,' said Mollie. 'But look, Jim! Isn't that our summer house? Yes, it is! I can just see the weathercock on the top by the light of the stars. We're at the bottom of the garden. The poor old snow-bird couldn't quite get back to the lawn he started from!'

'He's changed into snow and nothing else,' said Jim. 'What a pity that blue feather got blown away.'

'Children, children, didn't you hear me call?' cried Mother crossly, from the window. 'What are you doing out there in the dark? You know you ought to be inside by the fire! Come in at once!'

Jim and Mollie picked up the cushion

and ran indoors. They tried to explain
to Mother where they had been, and all
about the magic snow-bird, but she was
too cross to listen. She just popped them
into bed, and left them.

But do you know, in the morning the
snow-bird was standing at the *bottom*
of the garden, and not in the place
where Father and Mother had seen
him the day before.

'There you are!' cried Jim. 'That just
proves we are telling the truth,
Mummy. How could he have got down
there by himself? That shows he *did*
take us last night, and couldn't quite
get back to the right place.'

'Don't be silly,' said Mother. 'You
moved him yourself when you went out
to play in the dark after tea yesterday.'

'Well, anyhow, I've got that Christmas tree seed that the snow-bird gave
me,' said Mollie. 'I shall plant it,
Mummy, and then you'll soon see we
are speaking the truth, for it will grow
into a proper Christmas tree, all
decorated with lovely toys.'

She ran out and planted it in her own little garden. Nothing has come up yet, because it was only a week ago – but wouldn't you love to see everyone's surprise when it really grows into a beautiful Christmas tree, with a fairy doll at the top, and engines, books, teddy bears and other toys hanging all over it?

The Pixies and the Primroses

Once upon a time the Fairy King complained that primroses were too pale a yellow.

'They are such pretty flowers,' he said. 'It is a shame to make them look so pale and washed-out. I would like them to be as yellow as the daffodils. The daffodils are beautiful with their deep yellow trumpets.'

'Your Majesty,' said Scatterbrain the pixie, bowing low. 'Will you let me have the job of painting all the primroses a lovely deep yellow? I and my friends can do this easily. I have a special sunshine paint that will be just the colour!'

'I don't know if I can trust you to do a job like that,' said the king doubtfully, looking at the little pixie. 'You know how forgetful you are, Scatterbrain. Why, only this morning you forgot to put any sugar on my porridge, and when I told you about it you shook the salt-cellar over the plate! If I let you do

this job you would probably paint the primroses sky-blue or something silly like that.'

'Your Majesty, you hurt me very much when you talk like that,' said Scatterbrain, going very red. 'All I have to do is to give out the paint to my friends, and by the morning the job will be done! Every primrose in the woods will be finished! You will be delighted!'

'Very well,' said the king. 'You may do the work, Scatterbrain – but do be careful!'

Scatterbrain was overjoyed. He called all his pixie friends and told them of the work the king had given them. 'Come to me tonight and I will give you each a pot of yellow paint,' said the little pixie.

So that night all the pixies went to Scatterbrain's house. He had been mixing his yellow paint that day, and had a big pot of it. He poured some into hundreds of small pots, and gave one to each pixie, with a nice new brush. Off they all ran to the woods.

'I haven't done anything silly *this* time,' thought Scatterbrain, as he emptied the last lot of paint into a tiny pot for himself. 'Won't the king be pleased in the morning when he sees the primroses as yellow as daffodils!'

The pixies set to work. They began in the middle of each primrose and painted very carefully. The deep yellow colour looked lovely.

They went on painting – and then they began to look rather alarmed.

Their paints pots were very tiny and only held a little paint. By the time they had painted all round the centre of the primroses there was no more paint left in anyone's pot.

And so, by the time the morning came, and the king went to walk in the wood to see what sort of job Scatterbrain had made of the primroses, he found that each of them had a pretty deep yellow centre – but that was all!

'Your Majesty, I didn't give the pixies enough paint,' said Scatterbrain, ashamed. 'Let me make some more and finish the primroses.'

'Certainly not,' said the king. 'You would only make another muddle of some kind! The primroses are quite pretty with a deep yellow bit in the middle. Leave them as they are!'

So they were left. You can still see the little bit of deep yellow paint in the centre of each one.

Pixie Pockets

Once upon a time the two pixie tailors, Snippit and Trim, were very upset because someone had come in the night and taken all their needles and their best pair of scissors. Their reels of thread were gone too, and they were in a great state because they had promised to finish a suit for the king that day.

'We've another pair of scissors,' said Snippit, 'but we have no more needles and no more thread. What shall we do?'

'We might ask the spider for some more thread,' said Trim. 'She has plenty to spare.' So they sent a messenger to ask the spider, and she came to them, and let them draw enough thread from her to fill two reels. She caught six flies in their shop, and that was her

payment.

'What about needles?' said Snippit. 'We do want such fine ones for this important work.'

'Zzzzzzz!' said a big bee who had blundered into the shop, thinking that the fine blue suit the pixies were making was a bright flower. Snippit was just going to shoo her out when he thought of a clever idea.

'Wait a minute, Bee!' he cried. 'Will you do us a favour?'

'Zzzzzzz! What izzzzzz it?' buzzed the bee.

'Will you give us your sting to use for a needle?' begged Snippit.

'What will you give me in return, Sssssnippit?' buzzed the bee.

'Anything you want,' said Snippit. 'Let us have your sting, and you can think of something in return – we will make you a coat – or a vest or a new belt.'

'I'll think for a while,' said the bee. She sat down and let Trim pull out her sting very carefully. Then she went to fetch a friend, so that both little tailors might have a needle and work together. The bees sat and watched the busy pixies and marvelled at their sewing. The stings made fine needles, and you should have seen Snippit and Trim sewing with them, making tiny little stitches with the spider-thread.

When their work was finished they turned to the patient bees. 'Have you thought of anything you would like?' asked Trim.

'Yessssss!' buzzed the first bee. 'I have thought of something we need

very badly. We want pockets to put the pollen from the flowers in. We collect that as well as honey, you know. Could you make us pockets, pleazzzzzze?'

'Of course!' said the pixies, at once. 'Where would you like them?'

'On our hind-legs, I think,' said the bee. 'It would be eazzzzzzy to put the pollen there!'

So Snippit and Trim set to work and made clever little pockets for each of the bees, and put them neatly on their hind-legs. The bees were delighted, and flew off at once to collect pollen.

The pixies' pockets were just right. The bees packed them full of pollen and then flew off to the hive. How all the other bees envied them when they saw their new and useful pockets. You can guess that one by one they flew off to Snippit and Trim and asked for pockets, too.

And now every bee has a pocket on its hind-legs and packs the pollen neatly there. Don't you believe me? Well, see for yourself!

The Silly Little Duckling

There was once a small yellow duckling who lived with his brothers and sisters in a farmyard. The old brown hen looked after the ducklings and was a very good mother to them. All the ducks obeyed her except the little yellow one.

He was very naughty. He would wander away by himself and talk to the other creatures in the farmyard and the hen was afraid that one day he would get hurt.

'Stay by me,' she said to the duckling. 'You are not big enough to wander about the world yet.'

'Oh, I *must* go and talk to those white ducks over yonder!' said the little duckling. And off he ran before the hen could stop him. The ducks were waddling down to the pond in a long line.

'Good morning!' cried the duckling. 'How are you this morning?'

The ducks looked at him and then looked away. He was too small to bother about.

'Take me with you!' cried the duckling eagerly.

'No,' said the biggest duck. 'Go back to the hen. You are a naughty duckling to come so far.'

That put the duckling into a furious

rage. He made up his mind to go with the ducks, no matter whether they wanted him to or not.

But the ducks grew angry, and suddenly they turned upon the naughty little duckling and pecked him hard. Each duck took one peck at him, and when they had finished, the duckling felt very sorry indeed. He ran back to the hen crying in anger.

'Oh, those horrid ducks!' he cried. 'They ought not to be allowed in the farmyard! They ought to be driven away! They ought to be cooked for the farmer's dinner! Ducks have no right to live in a farmyard, no right at all! They are the horridest creatures I know! I shall go and tell the farmer about them!'

So the silly little duckling boldly went to find the farmer, and when he saw him, he told him all he thought.

'You ought to get rid of those ducks!' he said. 'They are wicked creatures! Why don't you cook them for your dinner?'

'Well,' said the farmer. 'Come back to me in eight weeks, little duckling, and if you still want ducks to be cooked for dinner, I'll take you at your word. I'll cook every duck in the farmyard!'

'Thank you,' said the duckling, and he ran back to the hen, well pleased. But when he told her what the farmer had said, she laughed and laughed and laughed.

'What are you laughing at?' asked the duckling, surprised.

'Wait and see,' said the old hen. 'You'll know yourself in eight weeks.'

The eight weeks went by. The duckling grew and grew. He learnt to swim on the pond, and became a fine white duck. When the eight weeks were up, he made up his mind to go to the farmer and remind him of his promise.

But just at that moment he caught sight of himself in the pond – and how he stared!

'Good gracious!' he cried. 'I've grown into a duck! I'm a duck, just like the others! Oh my, oh my, how I hope the

The Silly Little Duckling

The Silly Little Duckling

farmer won't remember what he said! I should hate to be cooked and eaten!'

'Ha ha ha!' laughed all the farmyard animals. 'What a foolish little duckling you were, to be sure!'

And I think he was too, don't you?

The Tale of Scissors the Gnome

There was once a tiny old man called Scissors. He was a gnome, and if you measure out six centimetres on your ruler, and cut out a little man that high, you will know just how small Scissors was!

He carried a pair of scissors about half as high as himself, and with them he cut out anything his friends wanted. A snip of his scissors and a coat would be cut out. Another snip or two and a party frock would be all ready for sewing up. He was a wonder with his scissors was the old gnome.

There was just one thing he was afraid of and that was rather strange, for he was afraid of the rain. We love to feel the rain on our faces, but Scissors was terrified. One big drop of rain on his head and he would be knocked flat on the ground, for he was so small. Once a drop of rain had broken his arm and he hadn't been able to cut out clothes with his scissors for three months.

Raindrops were as big as dinner-plates to him! So you can guess that if it began to rain, Scissors would run for shelter at once. If ever he went out he took with him his green umbrella, which was ten centimetres round and covered him well.

And then one day, when he had gone to visit the elf in the garden-bed, somebody stole his umbrella. He had put it down for one moment whilst he cut out a pink dress and somebody crept up behind him and ran off with his precious umbrella!

Poor Scissors! No sooner did he miss his green umbrella than it began to rain! Plop! A drop fell on his head and sent him on his nose. Plop! One went on his back and took away all his breath. Plop! A third drop made him so wet that he looked as if he had been swimming for weeks.

'Help! Help! Lend me an umbrella, please!' yelled Scissors. But nobody was near except the elf whose dress he had been making. She was a scatter-brained little creature and didn't know what to do.

But nearby was a strong nasturtium plant, and the flowers called to Scissors. 'Pick one of our flat leaves! They will shelter you well. They are just like flat umbrellas!'

The Tale of Scissors the Gnome

So Scissors gratefully picked a leaf, held it by the stalk, and stood under it whilst the rain poured down. It made a wonderful umbrella, and Scissors was pleased.

'I'd like to do something for you, nasturtiums,' he said, when the rainstorm was over. 'What can I do? Do you want any dresses, coats or hats cut out to wear?'

'Of course not!' laughed the nasturtiums. 'We already have orange and yellow dresses to wear. But you might cut us a pretty little fringe in the centre, Scissors – a nice whiskery one.'

So the gnome took his scissors and cut a fine fringe in the middle of the flowers. And if you don't believe me, go and look! As for his umbrella, Scissors never found it, but he always keeps a stock of nasturtium umbrellas in water, ready for when he goes out. Isn't he funny and wise too!

The Girl who Bit her Nails

Hetty was a pretty, neat little girl, with nice wavy hair and bright blue eyes. You might have thought that her mother would be pleased to have such a pretty little girl – but there was one thing about Hetty that made her mother quite ashamed of her. Hetty bit her nails! So, instead of having pretty nails to match her pretty face, she had ugly finger-tips, with the nails bitten right down. Wasn't it a pity!

Now one day when all the children in the playground were having fun, a small brownie man poked his head over the wall. He threw a card to the children, grinned, and disappeared into the fields nearby. The children picked up the card in astonishment.

'Please come to tea with the brownies on Saturday in Blackberry Wood at four o'clock,' was written on the card. Well, wasn't that exciting!

So, on Saturday afternoon, all the children set off to Blackberry Wood. Their hands were clean, their hair was brushed, they had on their best dresses and shorts, for the boys were going as well as the girls. The brownies were waiting for them, and the little men greeted them smilingly and led them to a big table for tea. The children sat down and wondered what sort of food they would have to eat – for there was none on the table!

'We are going to give you each your favourite food to eat,' said the brownies. They went behind each child, whispered a magic word over the plates – and lo and behold, what wonderful things appeared!

'I've got my favourite treacle pudding!' cried Jimmy, in joy.

'I've got cream cakes – six of them!' squealed Annie.

'I've got chocolate ice-cream – a whole plateful!' shouted John.

But what about Hetty? A most extraordinary thing appeared on her plate – a collection of nails! Yes, really! Big iron nails, little tin-tacks, small, thin nails, and fat, squat ones. There they all were on her plate, quite hard and uneatable. Hetty sat staring at them in dismay, and then she looked at the lovely things the other children were having.

'Eat up your tea,' said a brownie to

The Girl who Bit her Nails

her. 'We watched you eat your own nails each day, biting them whenever you had a chance – so we knew they must be your favourite meal. We couldn't give you nails like yours, so we've given you all the different sorts of nails we can think of!'

Poor Hetty! She went red and burst into tears! She jumped out of her chair and ran home, crying all the way. Her mother was quite worried when she came weeping in at the door. She listened to all that Hetty told her, and then she fetched the little girl a nice chocolate bun.

'The brownies didn't understand,' she said. 'After all, dear, you do bite your nails a lot, and of course they thought you loved eating them. Leave your nails alone in future and let them grow nice and long – then the brownies and other people won't make the mistake of thinking that your nails are your favourite meal!'

A Pair of Blue Trousers

Have you ever heard people say, 'It will be fine weather today if only we can see enough blue sky to make a sailor a pair of trousers?' We often say that, and we look anxiously upwards to see if there is just a little blue patch showing. I wonder if you know how the saying first began?

One year, long ago, there came a terrible spell of cold, cloudy weather. Not a patch of blue sky was to be seen. The weather-clerk was in a very bad temper, and he wouldn't send even a speck of blue anywhere. People were in despair, and couldn't think what to do. At last they went to an old wise woman who lived in her tumbledown cottage on the very top of Breezy Hill. 'Can you

tell us what to do?' they asked. 'We do
so badly want good weather.'

The old wise woman sat down in her
chimney-corner and thought for a
while. Then she said, 'If you can make
the weather-clerk put a patch of blue in
the sky big enough to make a sailor a
pair of trousers, the weather will turn
fine again. That is all I can tell you.'

Everyone puzzled over this, and no
one could think how to make the
weather-clerk put a little patch of blue
into the heavens. But at last a sailor-

77

boy stood up and grinned.

'I'll manage it for you!' he said. 'I've heard that the weather-clerk keeps a snappy dog outside his house. I'll pay the clerk a visit and see if his dog will snap a hole in my trousers. Then I'll go in and demand a new pair, and see what I can get out of him!'

So off he went – and you should have heard him growl at the snappy dog, who, of course, growled back, and flew at the sailor's trousers. It wasn't long before there was a big hole in them! The sailor-boy marched up to the front door and crashed the knocker down several times. The door flew open and the weather-clerk looked out angrily. But before he could speak, the sailor began to shout at the top of his voice:

'Look here, look here! See the hole your dog has made in my trousers! You want that dog locked up! He is a dangerous animal! You must pay me five golden pounds for my trousers so that I may get a new pair!'

'Nonsense,' said the clerk, and made

A Pair of Blue Trousers

as if he would shut the door. But the sailor put his foot in so that he couldn't, and began to shout again, so that the clerk was absolutely terrified.

'Be quiet, pray be quiet,' he begged. 'You are noisier than a thunderstorm. I have no money to give you for a new pair of trousers.'

'Well, I *must* have a pair!' roared the sailor. 'Give me a bit of blue sky to make myself a new pair. Then I will not charge you anything. Quickly, now, before I fetch the policeman to your dog!'

The weather-clerk, shivering and shaking, pulled two clouds apart, and a bit of blue sky peeped between them. The sailor thanked him, and ran off in glee. 'Look at the blue sky, look at it!' everyone cried in delight. 'The first we have seen for months!'

'Yes, *I* got it for you!' said the sailor-boy. 'I won't use it for my trousers, because you need it for good weather. But please buy me a new pair!'

So they did – and now, on a cloudy

day, look up into the sky, and see if you can spy a bit of blue big enough to make a sailor a pair of trousers! If you can, you'll see good weather before long!

The Blackbirds' Secret

Did you know that the blackbird family have a secret that they never tell any other bird or any other creature?

Hundreds of years ago the Prince of White Magic wanted to mend his Well of Gold. This was a strange and curious well, which, so long as history tells, had always been full of pure golden water. Anything that was dipped into this water became as bright and shining as gold, and was beautiful to see. But, because of so many, many years of usage, the well water had become poor and no longer seemed to have the golden power it once used to have.

So the prince decided to go to the Land of Sunlight, and buy enough pure golden rays to make his well golden again. He set off, taking with him a special thick sack so that the sunlight would not be able to shine through the sack and so give away his secret. He bought what he wanted, and by his enchantment imprisoned the sunny gold in the sack. He tied it up tightly and set off home again.

But somehow his secret journey to the Land of Sunlight became known, and the Yellow-Eyed Goblins, who lived in the Dark Forest, decided to waylay the prince as he passed

through their kingdom and rob him of the sack. Then they would use it for the Dark Forest, and make it light and beautiful.

Now the prince had made himself invisible, but he could not make the sack unseen. Also, much to his dismay, he found that it was not thick enough, after all, to stop the golden rays from shining through. He would very easily be seen in the Dark Forest. What was he to do?

He called a blackbird to him and asked his advice, and the bright-eyed bird thought of a splendid idea at once. He would ask each blackbird in the forest to spare a black feather from his wing and, with the help of the sticky glue that covered the chestnut buds on the trees, they would stick the dark feathers all over the sack, and so hide the brightness inside.

In a second this was done. The blackbirds dropped their feathers beside the prince and he rubbed each one in chestnut glue. Soon he had entirely

The Blackbirds' Secret

covered the sack with the black feathers, and it was impossible to see it in the darkness of the gloomy forest. He passed safely through the kingdom of the Yellow-Eyed Goblins, for not one of those crafty little creatures caught a glimpse of either the prince or his black-feathered sack.

The sunlight gold was emptied into the old well, and at once the water gleamed brightly. Anything dipped into it became a shining orange-gold, beautiful to see. The prince was delighted. He called the kind blackbirds to him and spoke to them.

'You have helped me,' he said, 'and now I will reward you. All birds like to be beautiful in the springtime and wear gay feathers – but you are black and cannot beautify yourselves. Still, you may make your big beaks lovely to see – so when the springtime comes near, blackbirds, fly to this well and dip your beaks into the golden water. Then you will have bright, shining beaks of orange-gold.'

And every year since then the blackbirds have flown in springtime to the secret golden well, and have come back to us with shining golden beaks.

The Lovely Present

The little Princess Peronel had been ill. The king and queen were glad when she began to get better, and they hoped very much she would soon be happy and bright again. It was dreadful to see her looking so sad.

In the middle of November the princess had her birthday, and the king meant to make it a very grand affair.

Perhaps the princess will cheer up when she sees all her presents arriving, he thought. I will send out a notice to say that everyone must try to think of something really good this year.

As soon as the people knew that the king hoped for plenty of amusing presents for Peronel, they set to work to make them, for they all loved the little

girl. One carved a big wooden bear for her that could open its mouth and growl. One made a whistle from an elder twig that could sing like a bird. There were all sorts of lovely presents!

There was one small boy who badly wanted to give the princess something, but he couldn't think what. He had no money. He couldn't carve a toy. He couldn't even make a whistle. He really didn't know what to do.

Then one day he did a very strange thing. It was a windy morning and the last leaves were blowing down from the trees. The little boy went out with a small sack. He stood under the trees, and every time the wind blew down a gust of dry leaves he tried to catch one. All that day he worked and all the next. In fact, he worked for nine days without stopping, and by that time his sack was quite full!

Then, on the birthday morning, he set out to the palace with the sack of leaves on his back. Everyone wondered what he had! Hundreds of other people were on the way, too, all with toys and presents. But alas for the king's hopes! Not one of the presents made the sad little princess even smile.

Towards the last of all came the small boy with his sack. 'What have you got there?' asked the king, in surprise. 'A year of happy days for the little princess!' said the boy. He opened his sack and emptied all the dry, rustling leaves over the surprised princess. Everyone stared in astonishment.

'Don't you know that for every leaf

The Lovely Present

you catch in autumn before it touches the ground you will have a happy day next year?' said the little boy to the princess. 'Well, I have caught three hundred and sixty-five for you, so that's a whole year. They're for you, because I'd like you to be happy and well again – so here they all are! And, as this is the first day of your new birthday year, you must smile and be happy!'

And she did, because she was so pleased.

The New Year's Party

Once upon a time three children went to a New Year's party. They were very excited, because it was to be a late party, right up to midnight. They were to hear the New Year coming in!

Susan was nine. She was a selfish, rather greedy little girl, with a mouth that turned down instead of up. Claire was quite different. She had a smiling mouth, and she was always doing little kindnesses to everyone she met. She was Susan's twin. David was ten, a lazy little boy who always got out of things if he possibly could!

It was a lovely party. It didn't begin till nine o'clock, so all the children had had a good rest in the afternoon.

They had games and a delicious supper. Then they played hide-and-seek all over the house. This was great fun. The house was old and very big, full of strange passages and poky corners.

'Let's go and hide upstairs somewhere,' said Susan to the others. 'We'll hunt for a good corner, and no one will find us there.' So Susan, Claire and David crept away from the people downstairs and slipped to the upper part of the house. They went up and up and up, and at last came to a curious, lost little room that had a candlestick with seven candles burning in it. They peeped inside.

The walls were covered with strange pictures, very long but not very deep – just like strips of tapestry or embroidery. They showed children doing all kinds of things, working, playing, eating, drinking, helping one another, fighting, dancing, sewing – really, the children could hardly take their eyes off the wonderful pictures.

'What a pity to have them stuck away up here!' said David. 'Let's see

The New Year's Party

which we like the best.'

'This one is nice, but it's been spoilt by ugly colours here and there,' said Susan, pointing to one that had great streaks of purple and red across it.

'And this one is spoilt because it looks unfinished,' said David. 'Look, there are bits left undone! How funny!'

Suddenly they saw someone else in the room – someone with soft wings and a shining, radiant face. It was an angel!

'So you have come to see last year's pictures,' said the angel, smiling. 'This is the picture *you* weaved through the days, Susan – do you see where you spoilt it with bad temper and greediness – you made those ugly marks on it. And that is *your* picture, David – the one you called unfinished. When you were lazy you left bits undone and spoilt it.'

'Where's Claire's picture?' asked Susan, ashamed of hers. As she spoke there came the sound of a clock striking midnight, and at once a great shouting and cheering broke out downstairs. It was New Year! One of the pictures suddenly glowed brightly on the wall – it was a lovely one, with no ugly marks, no unfinished pieces.

'Ah! That's Claire's,' said the angel, taking it down and rolling it up. 'A beautiful year's picture, Claire. I shall take it back to Heaven with me.'

The candles went out. The room was in darkness. The three children crept downstairs. They did not say anything about the strange room upstairs with the pictures – but they remembered it. Would you like to see your picture, too? I wonder what it would be like!

The Boy who Wouldn't Bathe

Once upon a time there was a boy who went to the seaside with his mother and father and sisters and brothers. His name was Thomas, and he had two brothers called Jim and Peter and two sisters called Mary and Emma.

Their mother bought them a bathing-suit each, and their father said he would take them into the sea to bathe every morning. So, when the right time came, Thomas, Jim, Peter, Emma and Mary put on their bathing-suits and ran down to the water. They had paddled that morning, and loved it – but as soon as they got out into the sea above their knees, the water seemed to feel rather cold.

'Ooh! It's too cold to bathe!' said

Thomas, shivering. 'I'm not going to!'

'Come along!' called his father. 'Wade out to your waist, then dip under! It's fine once you're in.'

Jim waded out and dipped under. So did Emma. Peter took a little longer, but under he went at last – and Mary lost her footing and went under without meaning to! So now they were all wet except Thomas.

And will you believe it, Thomas was still only up to his knees in the water! 'I don't like it, it's cold!' he wailed. 'I'm afraid of the deep sea!'

'Very well,' said his father. 'Stay where you are. You are behaving like a baby, so you'd better stay where the babies stay – at the edge of the water!'

So Thomas stayed at the edge of the water. He thought he would fetch his boat and sail her – so he did. It was a fine boat – not one of those annoying ones that flop over on to their side and lie there – but a proper one with big white sails. It sailed upright, bobbing up and down beautifully. Thomas held it by a string.

And then the strong wind blew the string out of his hand! His boat floated away from him, away, away on the wind, out to sea!

'Oh, my boat, my boat!' wailed Thomas. But none of the others heard him, for they were all splashing and shouting. Nobody saw the lovely boat sailing away either.

'Come back, boat!' shouted Thomas. But the boat took no notice. It sailed on, right away from Thomas, out towards

The Boy who Wouldn't Bathe

the deep, deep sea.

Thomas waded after it, crying tears all down his freckled nose. He couldn't bear to lose his beautiful boat. The boat sailed on. Thomas waded out further. He was up to his waist! Did he feel the cold water? No – not a bit! He waded on and on – the sea was up to his shoulders – up to his chin – and then he *just* managed to reach that runaway boat and hold it firmly! A big wave came and Thomas jumped up as it passed him. A little salt water went into his mouth, but he didn't care! He had his precious boat!

'Daddy! Daddy! Look at Thomas! He's out deeper than any of us!' shouted Jim. 'He's braver than any of us!'

His father looked – and he *was* really astonished.

'You're too deep, Thomas!' he shouted. 'Go back! I thought you said you were not going to bathe!'

'I'm not bathing!' shouted back Thomas. 'I only waded after my boat!'

How all the others laughed! Funny old Thomas – wouldn't go out into the water with his brothers and sisters, but didn't think twice about going up to his chin for his boat!

'Your boat has taught you to bathe!' laughed Mary. And so it had – for Thomas wasn't a baby any more after that! He went in the sea every day.

Hide-and-Seek

Allan and Sally were playing in the garden together. Allan wanted to play pirates, but Sally wanted to play hide-and-seek.

'I don't want to play pirates,' said Sally. 'You're always the pirate and I'm always the prisoner. Let's play hide-and-seek. That's a good game.'

'Pooh! It's a silly game!' said Allan. 'I'm going in to find my kite if you won't play pirates!'

He ran off and Sally sulked for a few minutes, sitting in the old swing. Then she brightened up and smiled – Allan *was* playing hide-and-seek after all! 'Cuckoo! Cuckoo!' she heard.

'I'm coming to find you!' shouted Sally. 'I'll soon hunt out your hiding-

place!'

She looked under the lilac bush. Allan wasn't there. She looked in the shed and under a pile of sacks. No Allan. She looked behind the rain-barrel in the corner. Allan was small and could easily squeeze behind it – but he wasn't there.

'Cuckoo! Cuckoo! Cuckoo!'

Sally stood and listened. Wherever was Allan hiding? It must be some wonderful new place he had discovered. She really *must* find it! Off she ran again in the direction of the voice. It sounded as if Allan were at the bottom of the garden. He must have squeezed himself into the very middle of the yew hedge where it was thick. She looked and looked but no, he wasn't there.

Then Sally became tired of hunting. 'Come out, Allan, you've won!' she called. 'Where are you hiding? It's a very good place. Come out, and we'll play pirates now!'

Allan didn't come. Instead there came the call again, 'Cuckoo! Cuckoo!'

Then Sally stamped her foot in a rage and shouted, 'Allan! Allan! Don't be silly! Didn't I say I'd given up? Do come out and play!' But no, Allan didn't come.

Sally ran indoors, crying. 'Whatever is the matter?' asked her mother.

'It's Allan,' said Sally. 'He's been playing hide-and-seek for ages, and he won't come out when I ask him to. He's wasting all our playtime; it's too bad.'

Hide-and-Seek

'But, Sally, Allan's upstairs looking for his kite!' said her mother, surprised. 'He's been there for some time. See, here he is with his kite.'

Allan came in. Sally stared at him in astonishment. 'Weren't you playing hide-and-seek just now?' she asked. 'Well, who *was*, then? *Someone* kept calling "Cuckoo" just like you do!'

'Cuckoo! Cuckoo!' called someone outside – and then, how Mother and Allan laughed and laughed.

'It's the cuckoo-bird come back again!' cried Mother. 'Oh, you goose, Sally – you've been playing hide-and-seek with *him*!'

'She's a cuckoo, not a goose!' cried Allan. And I think she was, don't you?

Pins and Needles

Quick-Fingers, the pixie dress-maker, was chased one night by the red goblin. She ran through the fields panting and a small bush called to her.

'Quick-Fingers, hide beneath me! I will shelter you!'

So Quick-Fingers crawled under the small bush and stayed there safely till the morning. She slept quite soundly, though it rained. But the bush held its leaves over her and not one drop of rain wetted the pixie's frock.

She awoke to hear a munching, crunching sound. 'Oh dear, oh dear!' the little bush said. 'Here's that great donkey again, eating me as fast as he can. I shall never grow, I shall never

grow. As soon as I clothe myself with fresh green leaves, along comes the donkey or the horse or the sheep; they munch and nibble at me all day long!'

The pixie was sorry for the little bush. She took out the needle and spoke to the donkey. 'Donkey, stop eating this bush! If you don't, I'll prick you with my needle!'

The donkey didn't stop, so he got pricked. He brayed and ran away. The

little bush was surprised that he had
gone so quickly.

'What did you use to prick him
with? What have you got in that box
there?'

'Pins and needles,' said Quick-
Fingers. 'Oh, little bush, if only you
grew pins and needles round your
leaves nobody would ever come to eat
you!'

'Do you know enough magic to grow
me some?' asked the bush eagerly.

'I think so,' said Quick-Fingers. 'I'll set pins and needles all round the edges of some of your leaves and sing a magic spell over them. Then they will grow and all your new leaves will grow pins and needles too!'

'Oh, thank you,' said the bush, 'then no one will ever want to come and eat me!'

The pixie did as she had said and then she sang a little spell. She said goodbye and went. 'I'll come back in a month and see how the magic has worked,' she promised.

When she came back, what a difference there was in the bush! It had grown well, for no one had dared to eat it.

Every leaf was set with prickles, as sharp as needles, as strong as pins!

'The donkey doesn't come near me! The horse is afraid of me! The sheep keep as far away as they can!' said the bush joyfully. 'Now I can grow big. I can grow into a high tree.'

'Well, mind you don't waste your

pins and needles if you grow tall,' said the pixie. 'No animal can eat your high-up leaves, so you needn't bother about pins and needles for them.'

Do you know what the tree is?

Guess! Yes, it's the prickly holly tree, and you've all seen how well its leaves are set with pins and needles!

And do you know, the tree took Quick-Fingers' advice and didn't grow prickles on its top leaves.

That's strange, isn't it? But if you'll look and see, you'll find it's true.

Just Big Enough for Him!

'I think I'll clean out my dolls' house this morning,' said Ellen to her Mother. 'I'll take it down to the shed, Mummy.'

Soon Ellen was very busy indeed. She carried her dolls' house down to the shed, and put it on the floor there. She opened the front of the house and set to work. First she took all the furniture out. Then she washed the floors and the walls, and shook the little carpets.

Then she cleaned all the furniture and put it back again. She made the two small beds, and wiped round the tiny bath.

'There!' she said. 'Now it all looks very nice. I think I'll leave it down here till I've washed the curtains.'

She took the tiny curtains back to

wash, and left the spick-and-span dolls' house in the shed. But it was dinner-time when she got in, and she hadn't time to wash the curtains. She popped them into the toy-cupboard and forgot all about them!

She didn't remember them till the next week. Then she washed them carefully, ironed them with her toy iron, and took them to the shed.

The door was open a little. She went inside and saw Blackie the cat sitting there, looking very solemn indeed.

'Why, Blackie – so it's here you come to when we miss you!' said Ellen, surprised.

'Miaow!' said Blackie. He pressed his face close against one of the dolls' house windows, exactly as if he were looking inside. Then he scraped at the front door, which was half-open.

'What are you doing?' said Ellen, in surprise. 'Blackie, surely you don't think you're small enough to get into my dolls' house! Take your paw out of the front entrance!'

'Miaow!' said Blackie, and put his paw in at the door as far as it would go. Then he put his face down to the doorway and sniffed hard.

'Really! Anyone would think you wanted to live here,' said Ellen, pushing him away. 'Cats don't live in dolls' houses!'

But Blackie wouldn't go away. He pressed his face against a window again. Ellen pushed him away once more and peeped in herself. What she saw there gave her a very big surprise!

Someone was in one of the little beds! Someone was curled up there, fast asleep, the tiny blanket half over him. Who could it be?

Ellen felt very excited. Her heart began to beat fast. Who had found her dolls' house and gone to sleep in one of the beds? Taking Blackie in her arms, she put him outside the shed-door and shut it. No wonder he was so interested in the dolls' house!

She opened the front of the house very carefully and looked into the bedroom. In one of the beds lay a small, furry creature, so fast asleep that he didn't even wake when Ellen touched him.

'It must be a mouse – or a kind of a mouse,' said Ellen, delighted. 'A very small, round one – and dear me, look at his long tail all curled round him. Oh, he's sweet! He's a pet! Oh, what will Mummy say?'

She decided to shut the front of the dolls' house and carry it up to her own house to show her mother. Blackie

was outside, waiting for her.

Mother could hardly believe her eyes when she saw the tiny animal in the bed. 'Why – it's a dormouse!' she said. 'What a pet!'

'Mummy, why doesn't he wake up? Why did he choose my dolls' house bed to sleep in?' asked Ellen.

'Well, it's autumn now and the cold weather has begun,' said Mother. 'Lots of tiny creatures sleep the whole winter through – and the dormouse is one of them. Usually they choose a hole somewhere – or perhaps the bottom of a flower-pot in a shed – but this one wandered into the shed and found your dolls' house door open and went inside. He curled up in the bed, the little dear!'

'Will he sleep there all the winter?' asked Ellen, delighted.

'Yes, if we keep him in a fairly cold place,' said her mother. 'You'll have to take your dolls' house back to the shed – it's cold there in the winter. He'll sleep well, then, and won't wake till the warm springtime!'

Ellen was so happy. To think of a dormouse choosing to sleep the winter away in a tiny doll's bed in her dolls' house!

'I'm lucky!' she said. 'Very, very lucky. I don't believe anyone else in the world has a dolls' house with a dormouse sleeping in it.'

I wish you could see him, curled up under the blanket, his tiny nose buried in his paws. He looks so lovely. I know because I saw him the other day. Won't Ellen be sorry when he wakes up in the springtime and runs off to play in the woods he loves?

The Lucky Green Pea

When Littlefeet was going down Twisty Lane, he saw a sack lying right in the very middle of the road. It was a large sack, and when Littlefeet looked into it, he saw that it was full to the top with peas in their pods.

'My!' said Littlefeet. 'Look at that! Someone's dropped it off his cart! I wonder whose it is.'

He lifted it on his shoulder, and found that it was very heavy, for he was not very big.

'I'd better go and ask Farmer Straws, in case it belongs to him,' said Littlefeet, for he was an honest little fellow.

So off he staggered with the sack of peas on his shoulder. As he went, one of the pea-pods burst, and a little green pea shot out of the neck of the sack, and dropped right down Littlefeet's neck. It tickled him a bit, but he didn't take any notice of it.

He didn't know that it was a lucky pea. It was the only pea in the whole sack that was a lucky one. It was lucky because a witch had passed by the row of peas in the night, and her broomstick had brushed against the pea-pod. A little mouse had eaten all the peas in it but one, and that was the pea that had dropped down Littlefeet's neck.

He soon came to Farmer Straws' yellow cottage, and shouted for him.

'Hey!' he called. 'Where's the farmer? I've got a sack of peas for him. He must have dropped it on the road.'

'It isn't mine,' said Farmer Straws, looking over the wall of the pigsty. 'But thanks for coming all the same. Look, Littlefeet, I've got twenty-one dear little pigs. Would you like one?'

'Ooh, yes!' said Littlefeet, delighted. 'I'd love it.'

So Farmer Straws gave him a pink pig with a curly tail, and he went off leading it on a piece of string. He carried the sack too, so he was well loaded.

These peas must belong to Mr Cabbage, the greengrocer, thought Littlefeet, staggering along under the sack. I'll go and ask him. He'll be most upset if he thinks he's lost them.

Soon he arrived at the greengrocer's, and Mr Cabbage came out to see him. He was feeding his hens in the backyard, and he was very surprised to see

Littlefeet with a pig and a sack.

'Have you come to sell me some peas?' he asked.

'No,' said Littlefeet, nearly putting the sack down on top of the pig. 'I found them and thought they were yours, so I brought them along.'

'That was kind of you,' said Mr Cabbage. 'But they're not mine. I haven't any at all. I sold a sackful to Dame Jolly this morning, and maybe they are hers. She took them away in her little cart, and I expect they've dropped off.'

'Oh, dear!' sighed Littlefeet. 'I had better go there then.'

'Wait a minute,' said Mr Cabbage, kindly. 'Have a drink of lemonade and a cake. And look, Littlefeet, do you see all my nice young hens? I've too many, so if you'd like one for yourself, you may take one.'

'Ooh, *thank* you!' said Littlefeet, full of joy. He sat down and had some home-made lemonade and a piece of ginger cake. Then, taking the sack on his shoulder again, he went off with the pig and the hen running beside him.

After some time he came to Foxglove Cottage, where Dame Jolly lived. He knocked at her door and she opened it.

'I've brought the peas you lost,' said Littlefeet, rather out of breath.

'I haven't lost any!' said Dame Jolly in surprise. 'I sold my sackful to the Haha Wizard who lives on Sailing Hill.'

'Bother!' said poor Littlefeet, putting the sack down, and just missing the hen. 'I felt certain it must be yours. I've tried Farmer Straws, and Mr Cabbage,

and now you!'

'I'm so sorry!' said kind Dame Jolly. 'Come in for a moment. I'm making some strawberry jam, and I'd like you to taste it.'

'Ooh!' said Littlefeet, who liked strawberry jam better than any other kind. He went indoors, wiped his feet, and waited till Dame Jolly had put some jam into a saucer for him. He ate it with a spoon. It was simply delicious.

'Nicest jam I've ever tasted in my life!' he said.

Dame Jolly beamed with delight.

'You must take three jars with you,' she said. 'I'll make a parcel of them and tie them on the piglet's back, because you certainly won't be able to carry them.'

'Thank you very much,' said Littlefeet. So Dame Jolly wrapped three jars up tightly in some newspaper, and then tied them firmly on to the piglet's back. He squealed and jumped about, but soon he was used to the load and trotted beside Littlefeet quite happily. The hen went too, and Littlefeet called goodbye to Dame Jolly.

In an hour's time he arrived at Haha Wizard's, and thumped at the door. The Wizard came to the door, and peeped out.

'Here are your peas,' said Littlefeet. 'You must have dropped them in the road.'

'So I did, so I did,' said the Wizard. 'Well, I wanted them to put into a spell, but I've done without them now. I don't like peas for eating, so I wonder if you'd

mind keeping them yourself?'

'Ooh!' said Littlefeet, who simply loved peas for dinner. 'Yes, I'd love to have them, and thank you very much!'

'Not at all, not at all!' said the Haha Wizard. 'You're doing me a kindness, I assure you. Good day!'

He shut the door and Littlefeet staggered off again, full of delight. This time he went home.

The piglet carried the jam in a very jaunty manner and the hen ran along beside him.

When he got home it was tea-time. He had spent the whole day carrying the heavy sack about! He had had no dinner, and he felt very hungry.

I'll cook myself a whole lot of peas! he thought. They will make a lovely meal. Just fancy, I've got enough peas to last me a whole week and more. Oh, what a lucky pixie I am! And I've got three jars of new strawberry jam, a little pig, and a nice little hen. This *has* been a lucky day.

He soon had a fine tea ready. There were green peas cooking, a new loaf, the strawberry jam, and a pot of tea. And then, would you believe it, the little hen laid him a nice brown egg!

'Just what I want!' cried Littlefeet, joyfully, and he boiled it for his tea.

When he undressed that night the little lucky pea fell out and rolled down a crack in the floor.

'What was that?' wondered Littlefeet. 'It can't have been a button, because they're all on. Oh, I'm sure it wasn't anything that mattered!'

The Lucky Green Pea

He didn't even look for it, which was a pity – but still, he had had enough luck to last him for a whole year, and there wasn't a happier little pixie in all the village that night than Littlefeet. He fell asleep, and dreamt of green peas and strawberry jam, little hens and little pigs – and when he woke up and remembered that his dreams were true, he chuckled very loudly indeed!

Bobbo's Magic Stocking

Once upon a time, many years ago, there was a little boy called Bobbo. He lived with his father and mother in a nice house in London, and he had plenty of toys and plenty of pets.

In the house he had his puppy, Jock, and his kitten, Snowball, and two yellow canaries. In the garden he had two pet rabbits, and a chicken that laid him a brown egg every morning as regular as clockwork.

In the nursery was a tall rocking-horse and a bookcase with twenty books of adventure and fairy tales in it. In the toy cupboard were balls, railway trains, bricks, teddy bears, clowns, a box of paints, and a cricket bat. So you wouldn't think that Bobbo wanted any-

thing else at all, would you?

But he did! He was always wanting something new. He was always tired of what he had got.

'Mummy, buy me this,' he would say; or, 'Daddy, buy me that!'

'You've got quite enough things,' said his parents, but more often than not they were foolish enough to buy Bobbo what he wanted, so that his toy cupboard was full almost to bursting.

The worst of it was that Bobbo would never give any of his toys away unless he was made to. He was a selfish little boy, who couldn't really be bothered to think about anybody else.

'I don't know how to cure him,' said his mother with a sigh.

'And I don't know how to cure him,' said his father with a frown.

But he *was* cured, and you will soon see how.

It happened that one night, about a week before Christmas Day, Bobbo was in bed, and couldn't get to sleep. He tried and he tried, but it was no use. He heard the clock in the hall strike nine, and ten, and then he heard his father and mother come up to bed. After a long time the clock struck eleven, and Bobbo knew that in an hour's time it would be midnight.

Fairies and elves come out at midnight, he thought to himself. I've never been awake at twelve o'clock before, so perhaps I may see or hear something surprising. I'll listen.

He lay in bed and listened to the sounds of the night. He heard the wind come whistling in at his window, and an owl hoot loudly. Then he heard another sound, a curious one that made him sit up, feeling puzzled.

It was the sound of sleigh bells,

jingling in the distance! Nearer they came and nearer, and Bobbo jumped out of bed and ran to the window. It was a bright moonlight night, and he could see quite well down the snowy street. First of all, in the distance, he saw something coming along that looked like a carriage drawn by horses. And then he saw what it really was!

It was Santa Claus's sleigh, drawn by four fine reindeer with great branching antlers! The bells on the reins jingled loudly, but the reindeer themselves made no noise as they trotted along in the deep snow. Driving them was a large elf, and at the back, in the big sleigh, was a crowd of laughing children, all in their nightclothes, the boys in pyjamas and the girls in their frilly nightdresses.

Bobbo stared in astonishment. The sleigh came nearer and nearer, and then, just outside Bobbo's gate, it stopped. The elf threw the reins on to the backs of the reindeer, and then took up a big book and opened it. He

Bobbo's Magic Stocking

ran his finger down a page, and then nodded his head as if he had found what he wanted.

He stepped down from the sleigh, and ran through the gate of the house next to Bobbo's.

Oh, he's gone to fetch Nancy from next door, thought Bobbo. I suppose he's fetching all the children who have been extra good, to take them for a trip to Fairyland, or somewhere. Well, I'm sure he won't fetch me, because I know I haven't been good for quite a week. Still, I don't see why I shouldn't go and have a look at that sleigh. I'm quite certain it's the one that Santa Claus uses and I don't expect I'll ever get another chance of seeing it so close.

He put on his slippers, and ran down the stairs. He slipped the bolts of the front door, and then opened it. Out he went into the moonlight, feeling not in the least cold, for it was fairy weather that night.

Bobbo saw that the elf had not yet come back from the house next door, so he ran down the path to his front gate. He saw that the sleigh was a very big one, and that the reindeer were the loveliest he had ever seen.

As he ran up, the children in the sleigh leaned out and saw him. They waved happily to him, and called him.

'Come along,' they said. 'Have you been a good boy, too?'

Bobbo stopped and looked at the children in the sleigh. He saw that they thought he was one of the good children that the elf was fetching. Quick as a flash Bobbo made up his mind to let them go on thinking so, for he thought that perhaps he would be able to go with them on the trip, if the elf did not see that he was an extra child.

He nodded and laughed to the children, and they put out their hands to him, and pulled him into the sleigh with them.

'Isn't it fun?' they said. 'Isn't it fun?'

'Where are we going?' asked Bobbo.

'Oh, don't you know?' said a golden-haired boy. 'We're going to visit the

place where Santa Claus lives, and see all the toys being made! He always sends his elf to fetch good children every year, and this year it's *our* turn!'

'Here comes the elf!' cried a little girl. 'He's got a dear little smiling girl with him! Make room for her!'

All the children squashed up to make room for Nancy. Bobbo got right at the back of the sleigh, for he didn't want the elf to see him, and he felt sure that if Nancy spied him, she might make some remark about him. Nancy sat down in the front, and began to talk to all the children in an excited little voice.

'Now we're off again!' cried the elf, climbing into the driving-seat. 'Hold tight!'

He jerked the reins, and the reindeer started off again over the snow, pulling the sleigh so smoothly that Bobbo felt as if he was in a dream. Now that he really was off with the children he felt a little bit uncomfortable, for he didn't know what the elf might say when he found that he had one boy too many.

The sleigh went on and on and on, through the town and into the country. At last it stopped again before a tiny little cottage, and once more the elf looked up his address book, and found the names he wanted.

'There are two children to come from here,' he said, 'and then that's all. After we've got them, we'll go straight off to the home of Santa Claus, and see all the wonderful things he has to show you!'

He went through the gate and tapped softly at the door of the cottage. It was opened at once, and Bobbo saw two excited children standing there, one a girl and one a boy.

'Come on, twins,' said the elf, cheerfully. 'The sleigh is waiting.'

The two children ran to the sleigh, and jumped in. The elf once more took up the reins, and the sleigh began to move very quickly over the snow.

'Hold on as tightly as you can!' said the elf. 'I'm going to go at top speed, for we're a little late!'

All the children held on to each other and gasped in delight as the sleigh tore along over the snow at a most tremendous rate. The wind whistled by, and blew their hair straight out behind them, so that they laughed to see each other.

'Look at that hill!' the golden-haired boy cried suddenly. 'It's like a cliff, it's so steep!'

Bobbo looked, and he saw a most enormous hill stretching up in front of

Bobbo's Magic Stocking

the sleigh. It was very, very steep, but the reindeer leapt up it as easily as if it was level ground. The sleigh tilted backwards, and the children held on more tightly than ever. Up and up went the sleigh, right to the very, very top, and then, on the summit, drenched in moonlight, it stopped.

'We've come to a little inn!' cried one of the children, leaning out. 'Oh, and here come six little gnomes, carrying something! What *are* they going to do?'

All the children leaned out to watch. They saw the gnomes come hurrying up, carrying pairs of lovely green wings. There were six pairs of these, and the gnomes knew just what to do with them.

Four of the gnomes went to the reindeer, and fastened a pair of wings on to their backs. The other two bent down by the sleigh, and the children saw that they had fastened two pairs of wings on to the sides of the sleigh as well!

'We're going to fly, we're going to fly!'

they cried. 'Oh, what fun it will be!'

When the wings were all tightly fastened the gnomes stepped back. The elf driver gathered up the reins once more, and the reindeer plunged forward.

Bobbo looked all round. He could see a long, long way from the top of the steep hill, and the world looked very lovely in the silver moonlight. As the sleigh started forward again he saw that, instead of going down the other side of the hill, they had jumped

straight off it, and were now galloping steadily through the air!

My word! thought Bobbo. Now we're off to Santa Claus's home! I do wonder what it will be like.

The sleigh went on and on for a very long time, but the children didn't get at all tired, for they loved looking downwards and seeing the towns, villages, lakes, and seas they passed over. The elf answered their questions, and told them all they wanted to know.

'Do you see that great mountain sticking up into the sky?' he said at last. 'Well, that is where Santa Claus lives. In five minutes we shall be there.'

Bobbo began to wonder if he would be found out by Santa Claus when he arrived.

Perhaps he won't notice, he thought. There are so many children in the sleigh that surely he won't see there is one too many!

Nearer and nearer to the mountain glided the sleigh, and at last it touched the summit. The reindeer felt their feet on firm ground once more, and the children shouted in delight.

On top of the mountain was built an enormous castle, its towers shining against the moonlit sky. Just as the sleigh bumped gently down to the ground, a big jolly man came running out of the great open door of the castle. He was dressed in red, and had big boots on and a pointed red hat.

'Santa Claus! Santa Claus!' cried all the children, and they scrambled out of the sleigh, and rushed to meet him as fast as they could. Bobbo quite forgot that he wasn't supposed to be there, and ran to meet him too.

The jolly old man swung the children off their feet and hugged them.

'Pleased to see you,' he said. 'What a fine batch of good children this year!'

Then Bobbo remembered. He slipped behind the twins, and said nothing. He was terribly afraid of being found out and sent home before he had seen all he wanted to.

'Come along!' cried Santa Claus.

'There's some hot cocoa and chocolate buns waiting for you. Then we'll all go and visit my toy workshops.'

He led the way into the castle. The children followed him into a great big hall, with a log fire burning at one end. Before the fire was a big fur rug, and the children all sat down on it, and waited for their buns and cocoa. Little brownies ran in with trays full of cups, and soon all the children were drinking and eating, talking and laughing in the greatest excitement.

'Now, have you finished?' asked Santa Claus. 'Well, come along then, all of you. We'll go to the rocking-horse workshop first.'

Off they all trooped. Santa Claus led them down a long passage towards the sound of hammering and clattering. He opened a big door, and there was the rocking-horse workshop!

It was the loveliest place! There were gnomes running about with hammers and paintpots, and everyone was working at top speed.

Bobbo's Magic Stocking

'Only a week before Christmas,' explained Santa Claus. 'We're very busy just now. I've had so many letters from children asking for rocking-horses this year that I had to have a good many hundreds more made than usual. Go round and see my gnomes at work.'

The children wandered round, watching the busy gnomes. Bobbo went with the golden-haired boy, and they saw the horses being carefully painted. One gnome was very busy sticking fine bushy tails on to the horses, and another one was putting on the manes.

Two little gnomes were doing the nicest work of all. They were going round the workshop, riding first on one horse, then on another, to see if they all rocked properly.

'How do you get the horses on to the sleigh?' asked Bobbo.

'Watch!' said the gnome he spoke to. He climbed up on to a rocking-horse and jerked the reins quickly. At once the horse seemed to come alive, and rocked swiftly forward over the floor before Bobbo could say 'Knife!' It went towards the door all by itself, neighing loudly, while the little gnome waved his hand to Bobbo. All the other horses began to neigh when they heard the first one, and the children stared in astonishment as they saw first one and then another come alive and begin to sway forward. Only those that were not quite finished kept still.

'Catch a rocking-horse and get on to its back!' cried Santa Claus. 'We'll let them take us to my next workshop — where the dolls' houses are made!'

Every child caught hold of a rocking-horse and climbed on to its back. Bobbo got a fine one, painted in red and green with a great bushy tail and mane. He took hold of the reins, and at once the horse rocked quickly forwards, following Santa Claus, who had jumped on to the biggest horse there. Off they all went on their strange horses, and rocked all the way upstairs to another big room.

'Here we are,' said Santa Claus. 'Now see how carefully your dolls' houses are made, children!'

The children jumped off their horses and stared in wonder. The room was full of little fairies, who were doing all sorts of jobs. Some were daintily painting the roof of a dolls' house, and others were cleaning the windows.

There must be thousands and thousands of houses, thought Bobbo, looking round. Oh, there's a fairy putting up curtains! I often wondered who put those tiny curtains up at the windows of dolls' houses!

He went round looking at everything. He saw curtains being put up, knockers being polished, pictures hung, and carpets laid.

'The fairies do all this because they're just the right size to get into the houses nicely,' said Santa Claus. 'Look! Here are some houses being lived in to see if they are quite free from damp, and have been well built.'

The children looked. They had come to one end of the big room, where a whole row of dolls' houses stood side by side. As they looked they saw the front doors open, and out came a number of little fairies.

'We sleep in the beds and see if they are comfortable,' they told the children. 'We cook our dinners on the stove in the kitchen and see if it is all right. We sit on all the chairs to see if they are soft. Then, if they are, we know your dolls will enjoy themselves here. And even if you don't let your dolls live in these houses, well, the fairies who live in your nurseries will often spend a night or two there, and they will be glad to find everything all right.'

Bobbo would have liked to stay there all night, watching the fairies pop in and out of the dolls' houses, but Santa Claus told the children to mount their rocking-horses again, and follow him.

'We'll go to the train workshop now!' he said. And off they all galloped again on their trusty wooden horses, downstairs and round a corner into a great yard.

'My goodness!' said Bobbo, when he got there. 'What a lot of trains!'

There *were* a lot, too! They were all rushing round and round, or up and down, driven by pixies.

'We've finished making all these,' said Santa Claus. 'They're ready to go to children now, but the pixies are just testing them to see that they run all right.'

Bobbo thought it was grand to test toy trains like that. The pixies seemed to be enjoying themselves immensely. They were very clever at driving their little trains, and never bumped into each other. They went under little bridges and past little signals at a terrific rate, their engines dragging behind them a long procession of carriages or trucks.

'Oh, they stop at the little stations!' cried the golden-haired boy. 'Look!'

Sure enough they did! There were tiny stations here and there with metal porters standing by trucks, and metal passengers waiting. And they all came alive when the engine stopped at their station! The porters began wheeling their trucks, and the passengers ran to get in the carriages.

'Oh, isn't it fun!' cried the children. 'How we wish we could ride in a little toy train too!'

'Very well, you can!' laughed Santa Claus. 'The metal ones are too small, but I've a big wooden train and carriages here that will just about take you all. Here it comes.'

The children saw a big red wooden engine coming along, driven by a pixie. It dragged three open wooden carriages behind it, and stopped by Santa Claus.

'Get in!' he said. 'There's room for all

of you. We'll go to the next workshop in the train and tell the horses to go back to their own place.'

At once the rocking-horses rocked themselves away, and the children climbed into the carriages of the wooden train. It was just large enough for them, and when they were all in, it trundled away merrily.

It took them to where the clockwork toys were made, and after that to where the red gnomes were making fireworks. Then they went to where the dolls were made, and the teddy bears and soft toys. And soon they had visited so many exciting places that Bobbo began to lose count, and became more excited than ever.

But at last they came to the only place they hadn't seen. This was a big room, in the middle of which a beautiful fairy was sitting. She sat by a well that went deep down into the mountain, so deep that no one knew how deep it was. No one had ever heard a stone reach the bottom.

'Now this,' said Santa Claus, 'is the Wishing Well.'

All the children looked at it in awe.

None of them had seen a wishing well before, and the fairy by it was so beautiful that she almost dazzled their eyes.

'All the good children who come here year by year,' said Santa Claus, 'visit this Well before they go back home. The fairy who owns it gives them one wish. She will give you each one, so think hard before you wish, for whatever your wish is it will come true.'

The children stared at each other, and thought of what they would wish. Then one by one they stepped forwards. The fairy handed them each a little blue stone, and told them to drop it into the Well as they spoke their wish.

The golden-haired boy wished first.

'I wish that my mother may get well before Christmas,' he said.

Then came the twins and they wished together.

'We wish our father could get some

work to do,' they wished.

Then came other children, all wishing differently.

'I wish my mummy had lots of nice things for Christmas,' said one.

'I wish my little brother may not be lame any more,' said another.

'I wish all the poor children in my town a big Christmas pudding on Christmas Day,' said a third.

So the wishes went on, until it came to Bobbo's turn. He had been thinking very hard what he would wish for, and being a selfish little boy, he thought of nobody but himself.

He went up to the fairy, and took the blue stone she held out to him. Then he turned to the Well, and dropped it in.

'I wish that on Christmas Day I may have a Christmas stocking that will pour out toys and pets for me without stopping!' he said.

At once there was a dead silence. Everybody stared at Bobbo, and he began to feel uncomfortable.

Then the fairy spoke sadly.

'Alas!' she said. 'I have given a wish to a child who is not good, for he is selfish. He will regret his wish on Christmas Day.'

'No, I shan't,' said Bobbo, feeling very glad to think that his wish wasn't going to be taken from him.

'Come here,' said Santa Claus sternly to Bobbo. The little boy went over to him, and Santa Claus looked at him closely.

'You are not one of this year's good children,' he said. 'How did you get

here?'

Bobbo hung his head and told him. Santa Claus frowned heavily, and all the watching children trembled.

'You have done a foolish thing,' said Santa Claus, 'and your own foolishness will punish you.' Then he turned to the other children.

'It is time to return home,' he told them. 'We are late, so we will not go by the reindeer sleigh this time. The fairy will wish a wish for you.'

'Come near to me,' said the fairy in her silvery voice. 'Take hands, all of you, and sit down on the ground. Shut your eyes and listen to me.'

They all did as they were told, Bobbo too, and shut their eyes to listen. The fairy began to sing them a dreamy, sleepy song, and soon every child's head fell forward, and one by one the children slept.

Bobbo's head dropped forward on to his chest as he heard the fairy's dreamy voice, and soon he was dreaming. He went on dreaming and dreaming and dreaming, and whilst he was dreaming, the fairy, by her magic, took him, and all the other children, back to their far-away beds. But how she did it neither I nor anyone knows.

When Bobbo woke up the next morning he rubbed his eyes, and suddenly remembered his adventures of the night before.

I don't think it *could* have been a dream, he thought. What about my slippers? I had those on, and if they are dirty underneath then I shall know I really *did* go out in the snow with them on!

He jumped out of bed and went to find his slippers. They were standing by the bed, and when he picked them up, he saw that underneath they were not only dirty, but wet too.

'That just proves it!' said Bobbo, in delight. 'Now I shall only have to wait a few days more for my wish to come true. Fancy having a stocking that will pour me out pets and toys without stopping!'

He told nobody about his adventure, and waited impatiently for Christmas Day to come. He wondered where he would find the stocking, and he decided that it would probably be hanging at the end of the bed, where Christmas stockings usually hang.

At last Christmas Eve came. Bobbo went to bed early so that Christmas Day would come all the sooner. He lay for a long time without going to sleep, for he was feeling very excited.

Then at last his eyes closed and he fell asleep. The night flowed by, and dawn came.

Bobbo woke up about seven o'clock and found a grey light in his bedroom. Day had hardly yet come. He remembered at once what was to happen, and he sat up quickly, his heart thumping in excitement. He gazed at the end of his bed, and saw there the Christmas stocking that his father and mother had given him, full of toys. Down on the floor beside it were lots of parcels, but Bobbo didn't feel a bit interested in them. He wanted to see where the magic stocking was.

Then he saw it. It was a little blue stocking, just the colour of the stone he had thrown down the Wishing Well. It hung on one of the knobs of his bed, and looked as thin and empty as his own stocking did, lying on the chair near by.

'Oh!' cried Bobbo in disappointment. 'Is that all my magic stocking is going to be?'

He reached over to the foot of the bed, and took the stocking down. Then

he had a good look at it. It was tied up at the top with a piece of blue ribbon, and the stocking itself felt as empty as could be.

'There's nothing in it at all!' said Bobbo angrily. 'That fairy told a story!'

He took hold of the ribbon that tied up the top of the stocking, and jerked it undone. It came off the stocking and fell on to the bed. Bobbo turned the stocking upside down, and shook it out on to the pillow, thinking there might perhaps be some little thing inside it.

And then the magic began to work! For out of the stocking suddenly came a kitten that fell on the pillow and began to mew! Then came a box of soldiers, and then a book. Bobbo had no time to look at each thing carefully, for before he had time to pick it up, something else came!

'It's working, it's working!' cried the little boy in the greatest excitement. 'Oh, my goodness, oh, my gracious, it's really, really magic!'

Out came a whole host of things on to

his bed! They certainly came from the stocking, though Bobbo could never feel them in there before they appeared. All sorts of things came, big and little, and even a rocking-horse suddenly fell with a thump on to the floor!

Soon Bobbo's bed was covered with toys. The kitten mewed as a ball came tumbling on to its head, and no sooner had it mewed than another kitten came falling down by it, and then a puppy and a little yellow canary.

After the canary came a whole string of white rats, about twenty of them. They ran about all over the place, and squeaked loudly. Bobbo watched them in amazement.

But then something happened that made the little boy begin to feel uncomfortable. The stocking suddenly jerked out of his hand, and began to flap about in a most curious manner, all by itself. Out of it came a long leg, with a hoof at the end. Then another appeared and yet another. The stocking jumped nearly up to the ceiling, and when it came down again, Bobbo saw that a great animal was miraculously falling on to the floor too. And whatever in the world do you think it was?

It was a great white donkey, with long black ears. As soon as it reached the floor, it began to make a most alarming sound.

'Hee-haw, hee-haw!' it went, and stamped on the carpet with its hind feet.

'Oh dear!' cried Bobbo, slipping under the blankets quickly. 'I don't like this. It's too much magic, I think!'

Now Bobbo's father and mother were lying in bed talking, when they suddenly heard the enormous noise made by the donkey in Bobbo's bedroom. Bobbo's father leapt out of bed at once, and his mother sat up in terror.

'Whatever is it?' she cried. 'It sounds as if it's coming from Bobbo's bedroom.'

'I'll go and see,' said his father, and tore down the landing. He flung open the door of Bobbo's room — and then

Bobbo's Magic Stocking

stared in the greatest horror and amazement.

And well he might, for Bobbo's room was full of hundreds and hundreds of things. Toys, big and little, were strewn all over the place, and kittens and puppies were playing madly together. White rats nibbled at the sweets and chocolates down by the bed, and a rabbit was lying on the hearthrug. Worst of all, the donkey stood with its forefeet on the mantelpiece, trying to nibble some carrots in a picture.

Bobbo was nowhere to be seen. He was safely under the blankets, cowering at the bottom of the bed. The stocking lay on the floor, and things jerked themselves out without stopping. Even as Bobbo's horrified father looked, he saw a tortoise come wriggling out, and make its way to where he stood on the mat.

'Oh! Oh!' cried Bobbo's father. 'What is happening here? Bobbo, Bobbo, where are you? Where have you gone?'

Bobbo answered from the bottom of

the bed.

'I'm here,' he said. 'Oh, Daddy, is it you? Come and rescue me from all these things.'

His father stepped over six white rats, stumbled over the rabbit, went round the rocking-horse, trod on a box of fine soldiers, and reached Bobbo. He picked up the little boy, blanket and all, and lifted him up in his arms. Then, nearly falling over a pile of big teddy bears, and squashing two boxes of chocolates, he managed to make his way safely to the door. He carried Bobbo into his mother's room, and told his astonished wife what he had seen.

Even as he spoke, two white rats ran into the room, and Bobbo's mother shrieked in horror. Then the donkey was heard falling downstairs, and two screams from below told the parents that the cook, and the housemaid, had seen him.

'What does it all mean, what does it all mean?' cried Bobbo's mother. 'Are we dreaming, or is this all real?'

'Bobbo, do you know anything about this?' asked his father. 'How did it all begin?'

Bobbo began to cry, and in between his tears he told the story of how he had been to the home of Santa Claus, pretending to be one of the good children. He told about his wish, and how it had come true that very morning.

'It's all that horrid magic stocking,' wept Bobbo. 'It's lying in my room jerking out things without stopping, just as I wished it to. Oh, why didn't I wish an unselfish wish like all the other children did?'

Bobbo's mother and father listened to the story gravely. They were grieved to think their little boy had not been good enough to be chosen, but had gone all the same, and wished a wish that showed what an unpleasant child he was.

'It's our fault really,' said his father to his mother. 'We have spoilt him, you and I. We have always let him think of himself and never of other

people. We must alter all that now.'

'I want to alter it,' said Bobbo. 'I want to be good, but I shan't have a chance now. That horrid stocking will go on and on all my life long!'

'Oh, bless us all, I'd forgotten that stocking would still be going on,' said his father, jumping up. 'Hello, what's that?'

He heard a loud voice shouting up the stairs. It was a policeman!

'Hi, there!' called the deep voice. 'What are you doing, letting your pets out of the house like this? You're frightening all the neighbours! This is a fine sort of Christmas morning to give them. Why, the road's full of puppies, rats, and kittens, to say nothing of rabbits, goats, and a snake or two.'

'Now I shall be put into prison!' wept Bobbo, more frightened than ever.

Bobbo's father waded through pets and toys until he got downstairs. There he saw the indignant policeman, and found that the cook and the housemaid had run out of the house in fright, and had left the front door open, so that all the pets had been able to wander downstairs and outside.

'Are you thinking of starting a zoo?' asked the puzzled policeman, trying to catch a white rat that was running up his trouser leg.

'No,' said Bobbo's father, 'it's magic, I'm afraid.'

'Come on, now!' said the policeman. 'You can't spin a story like that to me!'

A large swan came flying down the stairs and landed on his shoulder. He was so astonished that he fell straight down the front steps with the swan on top of him, and just as he was getting up, something got between his legs, and he sat down on a hedgehog.

That was enough for the policeman. Swans, snakes, hedgehogs, and rats seemed to belong to nightmares, not to Christmas morning, so he got off the hedgehog, and ran for his life to the nearest police station.

'Oh, my!' said Bobbo's father, seeing

two large tortoises coming solemnly towards him. 'That stocking must certainly be stopped!'

He ran upstairs, and went to Bobbo.

'How can you stop that stocking from sending out any more things?' he asked.

'I don't know,' said Bobbo, miserably. 'But perhaps Nancy, the little girl next door, might know. She was one of the good children who were taken to Santa Claus.'

Bobbo's father tore downstairs again, knocking over a duck on the way, and ran to Nancy's house. She was at the front door, watching the things coming out of Bobbo's house, and Bobbo's father told her everything.

'Yes, I think I know how to stop the stocking,' she said. 'Santa Claus told me, in case Bobbo was sorry about his wish. But is he *really* sorry?'

'He certainly is,' said Bobbo's father. 'This has taught us all something, and you may be sure Bobbo won't have a chance to be a horrid, selfish little boy again. He doesn't want to be, either.'

Nancy went to Bobbo's house straightaway. She picked her way through the animals and came to Bobbo's room, which was full right to the ceiling with toys and pets. The stocking was still performing on a mat near the door, and the little girl pounced on it.

'Where's the ribbon that tied it up?' she asked. 'Oh, there it is!'

She picked up the blue ribbon. Then she held the stocking toe downwards, and shook it violently three times.

At once a queer thing happened. All the toys and animals came rushing towards it, and one by one they took a jump at the stocking, and seemed to disappear inside it. Even the donkey vanished in that way, though Bobbo's father couldn't for the life of him think how. The stocking jerked and jumped as the things disappeared, and very soon the room became quite empty-looking. Still Nancy held the stocking, and then gradually the whole room, stairs and hall were emptied of their toys and animals. All the pets that had wandered into the street came back too, and at last nothing was left at all except the stocking, which lay quiet and still in Nancy's hand.

She took the piece of blue ribbon, and tied it firmly round the mouth of the stocking. Then she gave the stocking to Bobbo's father.

'There you are,' she said. 'It's quite safe now.'

'Thank you, Nancy,' said Bobbo's father, gratefully. 'I'll keep it in

Bobbo's nursery, just to remind of him of what happens to selfish children.'

He carried it in to Bobbo, and told the little boy what Nancy had done.

'Now you'd better make up your mind to turn over a new leaf, and try to be good enough to be chosen properly to go on the trip to Santa Claus's home,' he said.

'I will,' said Bobbo, and he meant it. 'I'll begin this very day, and I'll take my nicest toys to the poor children in the hospital.'

Bobbo kept his word, and tried his best to be different. He didn't find it

easy, but because he had plenty of pluck, he managed it – and you'll be glad to know that the very next Christmas he was awakened one night, and what should he see outside but the reindeer sleigh full of happy laughing children!

'Come on, come on!' cried the elf. 'You really are one of us this time, Bobbo!'

And off they all went with a jingling of bells over the deep white snow!

Gillian's Robin

In the winter-time Gillian put bread, potato and milk pudding scraps on the bird-table outside. The birds knew her well, and they sat round on the trees waiting until she had finished. Then they all flew down to the table to have a feast.

But the robin was so tame that he sometimes flew right down to the table whilst Gillian was putting the food on it! He sat on the edge at the back, put his head on one side and said 'Tirry-lee' in his chirpy little voice.

Gillian was fond of him. 'He is such a dear little fellow in his red waistcoat,' she said to her mother. 'I do love him. Mummy, perhaps he will build in a nesting-box if I hang one out for him.'

So her mother gave her a little wooden nesting-box and Gillian hung it in a tree, hoping that the robin would nest in it when the springtime came. He went and had a look at it, but he did not go right inside. He just sat on the top and said 'Tirry-lee'.

One day he brought another little robin to the bird-table. Gillian was so pleased. 'Mummy, Mummy, the robin has got a wife!' she called. 'Isn't she sweet? Oh, now perhaps they will nest in my nesting-box!'

Gillian spread food for the robins. She talked to them kindly and they listened. 'Please do nest in the nesting-box I have hung up for you in that tree,' she said to the two robins. 'I do want you to. It would make a lovely home for your children. You will be safe there. Please nest there to show me that you are my friends.'

The two robins went to look at the nesting-box. The little hen robin went right inside. Then she came out and said 'Tirry-lee' to the other. They flew off into the next garden.

Perhaps they are going to find leaves and moss to line the box with, thought Gillian, in excitement. So she watched and watched as she played in the garden. But they didn't come back, though she could hear them singing together in the next garden.

Poor Gillian! The robins didn't come near the nesting-box after that. It seemed as if they didn't like it at all.

'They don't trust me, perhaps,' said Gillian. 'They may think I will take their eggs or something unkind like that. Oh dear! I did hope they would put their nest in my box. Then I could watch them every day.'

She told her mother how disappointed she was. 'Never mind,' said Mother. 'They may have found somewhere they like better. Why don't you go and play in your little house and make it nice and clean for the springtime? I am having Old Thatch spring-cleaned. You can have your house done too.'

Now Gillian had, in the garden, a dear little house of her own that the gardener had built for her. It had one room inside, with a fireplace. There were two windows that opened, and a blue door with a knocker. It was a nice little house, and Gillian and her little sister loved to play in it.

Gillian took a pail of water, a scrubbing-brush, a cloth and piece of soap. She went down to her house and opened the doors and the windows. Soon she was busy spring-cleaning.

'I shall leave one of the windows a bit open so that the house will dry nicely,' said Gillian, when she was called in to her dinner. Then off she went, leaving the curtain blowing in the wind.

The next day was wet and so was the next. Gillian couldn't go down to her house to finish the cleaning. She did her painting instead, and sometimes she looked out of the window at the nesting-box, hoping and hoping that she might see a robin going into it. But she didn't.

The third day was very fine. Gillian put on her old coat and hat, took a duster and set off down to her house again. She opened the door. She looked at the floor to see how nice and clean she had made it–and to her great surprise it had bits of rubbish on it!

'Where could that have come from?' wondered Gillian. 'I suppose it blew in through the window. Well, now I'll do a bit of dusting and polishing.'

She was just going to begin when she

Gillian's Robin

189

caught sight of something in her doll's
cot. 'Good gracious!' said Gillian, in
surprise. 'There's some rubbish in my
doll's cot too. Leaves and bits of things. I
must clear it up.'

But just then someone came to the
open window. 'Tirry-lee!' said a chirpy
voice. Gillian turned to look. It was the
little cock robin, holding a leaf in his
mouth. He flew down to the bundle of
rubbish on the cot and tucked the leaf
into it. Gillian gave a loud squeal.

'Oh! Oh! You are making a nest! You're
making a nest in my doll's cot! You dear,
funny little robin, to think of such a
place!'

The robin flew out again. Gillian
rushed to her mother and told her.

'Well, darling, I should leave the nest
there,' said Mummy. 'It won't hurt the
cot, and you have no dolls there now. You
have only an old rug in it. Let the robins
make their nest there and have their
babies in the cot! They must trust you
very much indeed to choose your house
and your doll's cot to nest in!'

'They are my friends and I am their friend!' said Gillian, in delight. 'Oh, Mummy! I can easily watch them building.'

'Let them finish their nest in peace,' said Mummy. 'They won't be long. You can just see them hopping in and out of the window.'

So Gillian watched the two robins hopping in and out of the window of her little house, carrying dead leaves, grass roots, moss, and hairs that they had found in the grass where the dogs and cats had rolled.

'Mummy, the robins' nest is lined with some of Pat the cat's hairs, and some black hairs from Henry the kitten, and plenty of Rusty's and Skipper's hair!' cried Gillian. 'I wish they would use some of my hair too!'

Soon there were four eggs in the nest. The robins didn't at all mind Gillian and Fiona going in and out of the little house. The hen robin sat close on her pretty eggs, and the cock robin sometimes came in at the window or the door with a nice

fat grub for her. He sang 'Tirry-lee'
whenever he came.

The eggs hatched. Out came four tiny
black chicks. Then what a busy time the
two robins had! They had to feed their
four children all day long! Sometimes
Gillian found a grub and fed them too.
They weren't a bit afraid of her.

Then one day all the baby robins were
gone. They had flown out of the window
with their mother and father! Gillian was
sad to see the little nest empty.